From Silence to Song

L. Paula Scott

Copyright © 2025 L. Paula Scott.

All rights reserved. No part of this publication may be reproduced, stored in a retrieval system, or transmitted in any form or by any means—electronic, mechanical, photocopy, recording, or any other—except for brief quotations in printed reviews, without the prior written permission of the author.

Print ISBN: 978-1-944066-60-4

Published in the United States of America

Characters

Main Character: Faith Smyth, recently divorced Daughter: Kendra

Faith's Best Friend: Brooke Nichols

Choir members

Choir Director: Brandon Kelly

Potential suitor: Gabriel Laurent, Friend of Brooke and her husband James, successful lawyer

Prologue

She went into the bathroom, closed the door then looked into the mirror and opened her mouth and screamed. Well, screamed without making a sound. The silent scream. No one could hear it but she felt it resonating in her very soul. The hurt, the anger, the disappointment never failed to cause her to want to scream in frustration, yet she never wanted to frighten her daughter or cause her family to ask questions. That was the problem. She never wanted to cause anyone pain or concern, yet she herself was hurting. Today she met an old friend that caused her to think a lot about her life, the past, the present and the future. She was so tired of thinking and rethinking and over-thinking everything.

This is a new year; she willed it to be different than the last. For the past few years she has just existed. How she longed to live life! She longed for the abundant life that Jesus spoke of in the Bible. She felt stuck with no present options. This can't be what the Lord wants for His Beloved. How do you live abundantly in a situation that you've existed in for years?

Chapter 1
The Sanctuary

Faith pushed open the heavy oak door of the sanctuary, its hinges groaning softly, a familiar welcome. The setting sun poured through the stained glass windows. The fragmented colors danced across the floor and walls, creating a mosaic of light that seemed to pulse gently with life. She paused for a moment, letting the radiant glow wash over her, as if God Himself were reminding her of His presence. The scent of polished wood mingled with the faint hint of a refreshing lemon aroma, creating an uplifting fragrance that wrapped around her like a warm embrace. She exhaled deeply, her breath releasing the weight she carried every day—the silent battles that no one could see.

The stillness inside the sanctuary felt almost sacred, broken only by the faint hum of the fluorescent lights overhead. Faith hesitated for a moment, letting the calm settle over her. Slowly, she walked down the center aisle, her heels tapping against the wooden floor, their rhythm steady and grounding.

At the altar, she knelt, pressing her palms against the edge of the smooth, cool surface. The world outside seemed to dissolve, leaving only the whisper of her prayers. "Lord, give me strength," she murmured, her voice trembling, tears stinging the corners of her eyes but never falling. "Show me how to live, not just survive."

Standing, she made her way to the grand piano tucked to the side, her fingertips brushing across its gleaming surface before settling on the keys. Her first note rang out—a soft, reverent sound that seemed to echo through the empty space. As she sang, her voice gained strength, filling the sanctuary with waves of melody and longing. The words were her prayer, her plea, and her sanctuary all at once.

It was here, in this sacred space, that Faith felt closest to God—a bridge between her soul and His presence, woven from the threads of music and faith. It was a temporary reprieve from the chaos of her mind, a balm for her weary spirit.

The faint creak of the sanctuary door interrupted her moment, signaling the arrival of the choir. Faith turned, her expression immediately transforming into a bright, welcoming smile, her turmoil hidden behind a carefully constructed mask.

"Hey, y'all," she greeted, her tone light and warm as the group filtered in. Each familiar face brought with it a small sense of comfort, but she still felt the divide—her struggles were hers alone to bear.

Brandon, the choir director, approached her with his usual friendly demeanor, his clipboard in hand. "Faith, your voice is always a blessing," he said, his eyes full of admiration. "I'd like you to lead the solo for *His Eye is on the Sparrow* tonight."

The compliment brought a flicker of pride, but beneath it lay the familiar tension of her perfectionism. She nodded, smiling despite the apprehension that stirred in her chest. "Of course, Brandon. Thank you for trusting me."

As rehearsal began, Faith poured herself into the music, her voice soaring above the harmonies and weaving through the collective sound of the choir. Her passion for singing was unmistakable, a gift that brought joy to others while masking the ache she carried in her heart.

Chapter 2
The Encounter

The sanctuary was quiet except for the faint sound of Faith tidying up the hymnals after rehearsal. The soft rustle of pages and the occasional click of her heels against the tiled floor blended into the stillness. She didn't notice the figure at the door until a voice broke through.

"Faith, is that you?" Faith froze, startled by the familiar voice. She turned, her eyes widening in disbelief. "Brooke! What are you doing here?" Brooke stood in the doorway, her smile wide and warm, her eyes sparkling. Her black hair was styled in neat, intricate braids that framed her face, a little longer than Faith remembered, but unmistakably Brooke.

"I was in town and thought I'd drop by, taking a chance that you'd be here," Brooke said, stepping forward. "It's been way too long."

Before Faith could reply, Brooke wrapped her in a tight embrace, the years melting away in a moment. The sanctuary seemed to hum with the energy of their reunion, as if the space itself understood the significance of their bond.

They settled into a pew near the front, their conversation flowing with ease.

At first, it was light and nostalgic—the kind of reminiscing that felt like slipping into a well-worn sweater.

"Remember when we snuck into the park after dark? We were convinced we'd see something magical under the moonlight." Brooke asked, laughter bubbling up as she dabbed a tear from her eye. "We thought we were so brave."

"We were brave," Faith countered, giggling. "Cause if our moms had caught us! Whew! I still don't know how we managed not to get caught."

Their laughter echoed in the sanctuary, mingling with the fading light filtering through the stained glass windows. The kaleidoscope of colors reflected on their faces, like memories stretching across time.

As the evening wore on, their laughter gave way to heavier topics. Brooke's voice softened, her smile fading into something more reflective. "I've been through some tough times, Faith," she said, her hands clasped tightly in her lap. "There were days I didn't know if I could keep going."

Faith listened intently, her own heart aching as she heard Brooke recount her struggles—the loneliness, the fear, the moments when the weight of the world seemed unbearable.

"Besides my daily prayer and devotional time, journaling helped me,"

Brooke continued, her tone tinged with hope. "It gave me clarity, a way to sort through the chaos in my mind and heart. It became a tool for healing."

Her words hung in the air, resonating deeply with Faith. She could feel something shift within her, as if Brooke's story was unlocking a door she hadn't dared approach before.

"You should try it, Faith," Brooke said, her voice gentle but firm. "It's not magic, but it can help you find your way and gain some clarity."

Faith nodded slowly, her mind racing with possibilities she hadn't considered before. "Maybe I will. Thank you, Brooke. You've given me a lot to think about."

The two of them continued talking late into the night, their voices a quiet murmur in the vast sanctuary. Brooke's visit felt like more than a reunion—it was a turning point, a spark that ignited Faith's desire to change her own circumstances.

Chapter 3
The Revelation

The choir was in full swing, their voices intertwining in a symphony of hope and renewal. The notes soared, filling the sanctuary with a palpable energy, and Faith closed her eyes, letting the music envelop her. The hymn's lyrics spoke of new beginnings, redemption, and God's unwavering love. As the words echoed in her ears, something inside her shifted.

She felt it first as a warmth spreading through her chest, a sensation that radiated outward, softening the tension she hadn't even realized she was holding. The harmonies seemed to pierce through the walls she had carefully constructed, exposing the fears and doubts she'd carried for so long.

In that sacred moment, it was as if a veil had been lifted from her spirit. Her life lay before her with startling clarity, and for the first time, she saw the truth—how often she had held herself back, not because of others, but because of her own fear of failure and self-doubt. Tears streamed down her face, silent and unchecked, as she whispered a prayer that felt deeper and more earnest than any she had spoken before.

"Lord, help me," she prayed, her heart aching with the weight of her revelation. "Give me the strength to change, to become the person You want me to be."

As the final notes of the hymn faded into the stillness, Faith opened her eyes, her vision blurred by tears but her heart inexplicably lighter. A renewed sense of purpose coursed through her veins. She didn't have all the answers, but for the first time, she believed she could find them.

Later that evening, after rehearsal, Faith sat at the small desk in her room, a leather-bound journal lying open before her. The soft glow of the lamp illuminated its blank pages, and for a moment, she hesitated.

Brooke's words echoed in her mind: *Journaling helped me. It gave me clarity, a way to sort through the chaos in my mind and heart.*

Taking a deep breath, Faith picked up her pen and began to write. At first, her thoughts came in fragments, tentative and uncertain. But as the ink flowed, so did her emotions—her fears, her hopes, and the dreams she had buried beneath the weight of daily life.

She poured herself onto the pages, each word a release, each sentence a step toward healing. It wasn't just a recounting of events; it was a dialogue with herself, with God, a way to give shape to the swirling thoughts that so often overwhelmed her.

The more she wrote, the more she realized how much she had kept locked inside. Journaling became an extension of her prayers, a quiet time to reflect and seek guidance. With each entry, she felt a little more clarity, a little more strength to move forward.

The next day, Faith carried her journal with her, tucking it into her bag like a cherished companion. She had begun a journey, one step at a time, and though the road ahead was uncertain, she felt a flicker of hope. She wasn't alone—God was with her, and through her writing and her music, she was finding her voice again.

Chapter 4
The Challenge

The kitchen was dimly lit, a single bulb casting a soft yellow glow over the cluttered table. Bills and paperwork were scattered across its surface, an unrelenting reminder of the new reality Faith faced. She sat with her head in her hands, the ache in her temples mirroring the heaviness in her heart. The sound of the clock ticking on the wall seemed louder than usual, each tick marking another second of anxiety.

Her journey from stay-at-home mom to sole provider felt like a cruel twist of fate, one she hadn't been prepared for. The financial strain wrapped around her like an ever-tightening vise, and no matter how many numbers she crunched, the ends refused to meet.

"Mom, are you okay?" Kendra's voice broke through the silence. Faith looked up to see her daughter standing in the doorway, her face etched with worry.

Forcing a smile, Faith straightened in her chair. "I'm fine, sweetie. Just a little tired."

Kendra stepped closer, her eyes searching her mother's face. She didn't believe her, but she nodded anyway. "Okay… Let me know if you need help."

Faith's heart ached as she watched her daughter retreat down the hall. Kendra was too young to bear the weight of their struggles, yet the tension in the house had become impossible to hide. Faith felt like she was failing, not just as a provider but as a mother.

The rest of the evening passed in a blur of chores and forced smiles. By the time Kendra was in bed, the weight of the day pressed down on Faith with renewed force. She sank into the chair by her bedroom window, her journal resting on her lap.

Opening to a blank page, she stared at it for a long moment, the pen trembling in her hand. Then, as if a dam had burst, the words began to flow.

Lord, I don't know how much more I can take. I'm trying so hard to keep everything together, but it feels like I'm falling apart.

She paused, taking a shaky breath before continuing.

The bills keep piling up, and I'm so scared I won't be able to provide for Kendra. She deserves so much more than this. Please, Lord, show me the way. Give me the strength to keep going and the wisdom to make the right choices.

As the ink filled the page, Faith felt some of the tension begin to lift. The act of writing was like a release valve, allowing her to pour out the fears and frustrations she kept bottled up inside. She didn't have the answers, but for the first time that day, she felt a faint glimmer of peace.

Setting the journal aside, Faith whispered a prayer. "Thank You, Lord, for being my refuge, even in this storm."

She glanced over at Kendra's room, the soft sound of her daughter's breathing audible in the stillness. It was for her, Faith reminded herself that she would keep fighting. No matter how heavy the burden, she couldn't give up.

With that resolve, Faith climbed into bed. Sleep didn't come easily, but when it did, it was accompanied by a sense of quiet hope—a hope she hadn't felt in a long time.

Chapter 5
The Support

Every Thursday evening, the choir gathered in the sanctuary for their weekly rehearsal. The room was filled with laughter, shared stories, and a collective energy that carried them through the most complex harmonies.

For Faith, these rehearsals had become more than just a commitment to singing—they were a lifeline, a momentary escape from the chaos of her reality.

This particular rehearsal had been no different. The choir worked through their songs with determination and joy, their voices rising and falling in unison. Faith tried her best to focus, but her exhaustion was beginning to seep through the cracks she so carefully concealed. As they finished the final hymn and began packing up, Brandon, the choir director, approached her, his expression filled with concern.

"Faith, we've noticed you've been struggling," he said gently, his voice low enough to keep their conversation private. "We want to help."

Faith froze, her eyes welling with tears she hadn't wanted anyone to see. "I don't know what to say. Thank you," she replied, her voice trembling with gratitude.

The next few weeks brought a wave of unexpected kindness from her choir friends. They rallied around her, offering both emotional and practical support that eased her burdens. Word of her struggles spread quietly, and without hesitation, her community stepped in.

They organized a fundraiser, setting up tables at the church to sell baked goods and crafts, all proceeds going toward Faith's family's financial needs. They prepared homemade meals, delivered them with warm smiles and encouraging words, and even offered to look after Kendra when Faith needed a moment to breathe.

One Sunday after service, a choir member named Candice pulled Faith aside and handed her a bag filled with groceries. "You're not alone, Faith," she said, wrapping her in a hug that felt like the comfort of a prayer. "We're here for you. Always."

Faith couldn't hold back her tears any longer. She realized that the strength she had been searching for wasn't something she had to muster on her own—it was there, woven into the fabric of the people around her.

The weekly rehearsals took on a new meaning for Faith. The music seemed richer, the connections deeper, as she began to understand the power of community. The sanctuary wasn't just a place for singing; it was a refuge, a testament to God's love expressed through the kindness of others.

As Faith sat in her room one evening, her journal open before her, she wrote about the profound impact her choir friends had made on her life.

Lord, thank You for showing me Your love through these amazing people. I thought I was alone, but You've surrounded me with a community that lifts me up. Help me to be as much of a blessing to them as they've been to me.

Through their support, Faith learned an invaluable lesson: leaning on others was not a sign of weakness but of courage, faith, and humility. Together, they formed a network of care and resilience, a lifeline that carried her through the darkest times.

Chapter 6
The Decision

Faith stared at the stack of enrollment papers on the kitchen table, her heart racing with equal parts fear and excitement. For years, the dream of becoming a counselor had been a faint whisper in the back of her mind, something she dismissed as impractical and out of reach. But now, inspired by her friends' encouragement and her renewed faith, she felt the courage to take the leap.

"Mom, are you sure about this?" Kendra asked, her brow furrowed with concern as she looked up from her homework at the table.

Faith nodded, her resolve unwavering. "Yes, Kendra. It's something I've always wanted to do. I need to do this—for myself and for us. I want to show you that it's never too late to follow your dreams."

Kendra's lips curved into a small, supportive smile. "I believe in you, Mom," she said, walking around the table to give her a tight hug. "You can do this."

Faith's heart swelled with gratitude, and she kissed the top of Kendra's head. "Thank you, sweetie. That means the world to me."

Her decision wasn't without challenges. Balancing her new full-time job, Kendra's needs, and her coursework felt overwhelming at times. Some family members questioned her choice, offering unsolicited opinions about how she was taking on too much. But Faith held onto her sense of purpose, repeating a quiet prayer for strength every time doubt began to creep in.

It was during one of Brooke's family gatherings that Faith first met Gabriel Laurent. Brooke and her husband, James, had invited Faith and Kendra to a Saturday barbecue, a rare chance to relax and enjoy good company.

"Faith, there's someone I want you to meet," Brooke said with a knowing smile as she led her friend over to the patio. Standing by the grill was a tall, well-dressed man with deep brown eyes and an easy smile that immediately drew Faith's attention.

"Faith, this is Gabriel Laurent," Brooke introduced. "Gabriel is an old friend of James and me. He's a brilliant international attorney and business consultant—and he's fluent in several languages, as you'll soon hear.

Gabriel, this is Faith."

Gabriel extended his hand, his deep brown eyes meeting hers with warmth. "Enchanté, Faith," he said, his French accent soft but unmistakably charming. "It is a pleasure to meet you."

Faith shook his hand, momentarily caught off guard by the richness of his voice and the elegance of his accent. "The pleasure's mine," Faith replied, shaking his hand and feeling a surprising sense of ease despite her initial nervousness.

As the afternoon unfolded, Faith found herself drawn into conversation with Gabriel. His accent added an extra layer of magnetism to his words, turning even ordinary topics into fascinating exchanges. He spoke passionately about his work, his travels, and his belief in finding balance between ambition and meaning in life. In turn, Faith shared her journey—the struggles of her divorce, the decision to pursue counseling, and her faith that had carried her through.

"I admire your courage," Gabriel said, his tone sincere. "It takes strength to start over and chase a dream, especially when the odds seem stacked against you."

Faith felt the heat in her cheeks, flushing at his words, but she smiled shyly. "I'm just trying to take it one step at a time." "You are doing far more than that," Gabriel countered, his accent making the words feel like a melody. "And you will succeed—I am certain of it."

The hours passed quickly, and by the end of the barbecue, Faith realized how much lighter her heart felt. Gabriel had a way of listening that made her feel seen, something she hadn't experienced in a long time.

As the barbecue wound down, Gabriel approached her once more. "Faith, if you ever need advice—or even just someone to talk to—I would be delighted to help. Please, do not hesitate to reach out."

Faith nodded, her gratitude evident. "Thank you, Gabriel. That means more than you know."

That evening, as Faith wrote in her journal, she reflected on her decision to enroll in college and the unexpected kindness of strangers like Gabriel.

Lord, thank You for guiding me on this path and for surrounding me with people who lift me up. Please help me to stay focused and trust that You have a plan for me.

Her pen paused as she thought about Gabriel's words of encouragement before she added, *And thank You for letting me meet Gabriel. His words stayed with me longer than I expected.*

Though she wasn't ready to open her heart to romance, the idea of letting someone in—a possibility she had long closed off—didn't feel as impossible as it once had. Gabriel had sparked something within her—a quiet hope that maybe, one day, there would be room for both her dreams and her heart to grow.

This marked the beginning of not only a new chapter in Faith's life but also the subtle stirring of hope that perhaps the song of her heart was meant to grow richer, fuller, and more complete.

Chapter 7
The Journey

Faith sat in her first class, her heart pounding as she took in the unfamiliar surroundings. The room buzzed with youthful energy, the younger students chatting animatedly before the professor arrived. She glanced around, feeling a wave of self-doubt wash over her.

Am I too old for this? Can I really do this? she wondered.

But as the professor began to speak, the nerves eased, replaced by a spark of excitement. The lecture was invigorating, and for the first time in years, she felt like she was exactly where she belonged.

"This is it," Faith thought. "This is where I'm meant to be."

The journey was far from easy. There were late nights spent pouring over textbooks and challenging assignments that left her second-guessing herself. Self-doubt was a constant companion, whispering that she had taken on more than she could handle. But every time she felt like giving up, a small victory reminded her of why she had started.

Faith aced her first exam, earning a glowing remark from her professor: "This is exceptional work, Faith. You have a real gift." The words buoyed her spirits, fueling her determination. She began forming friendships with her classmates, who admired her dedication, and her professors, who encouraged her growth.

At home, her family began to rally around her. Kendra, who had always been perceptive beyond her years, would bring her tea during long study sessions or sit quietly nearby as Faith worked.

"Mom, you look tired. Can I help with anything?" Kendra asked one evening as Faith wrestled with a particularly difficult assignment.

Faith looked up, her heart softening at the concern in her daughter's eyes. "Thank you, sweetie. Just having you here helps more than you know."

While Faith juggled her responsibilities, Gabriel Laurent remained a steady, encouraging presence in her life. Since their first meeting, he had pursued her with a gentle sincerity that earned her respect and gradually gained her trust.

Gabriel would often call or send thoughtful messages, checking in on how she was managing her studies and offering words of encouragement. "How is my favorite student doing today?" he teased one afternoon over the phone, his French accent lacing the words with warmth.

Faith chuckled, appreciating his humor. "Trying not to drown in assignments, but I'm hanging in there."

"You are stronger than you think, Faith," Gabriel said, his voice sincere. "And if anyone can manage all this with grace, it's you."

Occasionally, he stopped by after choir rehearsal to catch up. One evening, he arrived with a bouquet of sunflowers. "For the woman who brightens every room she enters," he said, presenting them with an earnest smile.

Faith felt her cheeks warm. "Thank you, Gabriel. You really didn't have to do this."

"I wanted to," he replied simply. "You deserve to be reminded of how remarkable you are."

While Faith remained guarded, hesitant to open her heart fully, she couldn't deny the comfort and joy Gabriel's presence brought. His patience and unwavering kindness left an impression, planting seeds of hope she hadn't allowed herself to feel in years.

As the weeks turned into months, Faith continued to balance her studies, her family, and the growing connection with Gabriel. Each small victory—whether it was an exam she aced, a professor's praise, or Kendra's proud smile—reminded her of her strength.

One quiet night, as Faith sat in her room with her journal, she reflected on how far she had come.

Lord, thank You for this journey—for the lessons, the challenges, and the people You've placed in my life. Thank You for Gabriel, who shows me kindness when I most need it. Please guide me as I continue on this path.

She closed her journal, a sense of peace settling over her. Her journey was far from over, but with her faith, her family, and her growing support network, Faith knew she was moving closer to the life she was meant to live.

Chapter 8
The Transformation

Faith stood backstage, clutching her cap in her hands as she waited for her name to be called. The energy in the air was electric—an exhilarating mix of excitement, relief, and pride radiating from the graduates around her.

She took a deep breath, silently offering a prayer of thanks for the journey that had brought her here.

Her name echoed through the auditorium: "Faith Smyth, graduating Sigma Cum Laude!"

The applause roared as Faith stepped onto the stage. Her heart swelled as she accepted her diploma, the culmination of years of hard work, perseverance, and faith. She glanced into the crowd and spotted her family in the front row. Kendra was waving enthusiastically, her smile wide and bright, and next to her, Gabriel was clapping with an unmistakable pride in his eyes.

"Congratulations, Mom!" Kendra called, her voice carrying above the crowd.

Faith beamed, tears slipping down her cheeks as she waved back. "Thank you, sweetheart," she whispered, her voice thick with emotion.

The moment was overwhelming—proof of how far she had come. She had fought through fear, doubt, and challenges to pursue her dream of becoming a counselor. Standing on that stage, Faith finally felt the abundant life she had prayed for take root within her.

Faith's transformation didn't stop there. Just weeks after graduation, she received an extraordinary job offer from an international counseling organization. The position allowed her to work remotely, setting her own hours while offering support to clients from all corners of the world. It was more than she had ever dared to hope for—a chance to help others while creating a life of freedom and balance for herself and her family.

As Faith settled into her new role, she quickly discovered the profound fulfillment that came from guiding others toward healing and growth. Her virtual counseling sessions often ended with heartfelt thanks from clients who had begun to see the light in their own lives. The work was deeply rewarding, a testament to the strength that had carried her through her darkest moments.

Her relationships with her family and friends blossomed as well. Kendra flourished, inspired by her mother's determination, and Brooke remained a steadfast presence in Faith's life. But perhaps most surprising was the steady growth of her relationship with Gabriel.

Gabriel had pursued Faith with a quiet patience, never pushing, always respecting the pace she needed. He celebrated her achievements wholeheartedly, reminding her often of how capable and extraordinary she was.

"I told you," he said one evening over dinner, his French accent wrapping around the words like a melody. "You were always meant to do great things."

Faith chuckled, shaking her head. "You always know what to say, Gabriel." "I only speak the truth," he replied, his gaze warm and earnest.

Their connection deepened naturally, rooted in mutual respect, understanding, and their shared knowledge that God must always be first in their lives. Gabriel became not only a source of encouragement but also a partner in Faith's journey—a reminder that love, when built on trust and shared purpose, could bloom even after years of heartache.

One evening, Faith found herself back in the sanctuary where her journey had truly begun. She stood at the altar, looking out at the empty pews bathed in the soft glow of candlelight. Gabriel joined her, standing quietly by her side.

"This place," Faith said softly, her voice tinged with awe, "has seen me at my lowest and now at my highest. I can feel God's presence here more than anywhere else."

Gabriel took her hand gently, his fingers warm against hers. "It is because this place has been a part of your transformation, Faith. And you—you have been courageous enough to walk the path He laid before you."

Faith turned to him, her heart full. For the first time, she felt completely at peace—secure in her faith, her purpose, and the love she had found along the way.

Her story became a testament to the power of faith, community, and perseverance. From the depths of despair to the heights of triumph, Faith's journey was proof that God's plans are greater than what we can imagine. She had found her voice, her calling, and her song, living each day with gratitude and hope for what lay ahead.

As Faith walked out of the sanctuary that night, hand in hand with Gabriel, she looked up at the stars and smiled. The future was a beautiful, unwritten melody, and she was ready to sing it.

About the Author

L. Paula Scott is a storyteller, prayer leader, and encourager passionate about faith, healing, and personal restoration, whose mission is to help women rediscover their voices through faith. A devoted mother and mentor, Paula writes with honesty and hope about real-life struggles, healing, and the transforming power of God's love. She  draws from her own journey of heartbreak and renewal to encourage readers that even the quietest prayers are heard by a faithful God. Her writing invites readers to experience grace in the middle of their own silent seasons. She believes that every woman's silent scream matters to God, and that healing begins when we dare to speak—and to believe—again.

www.ingramcontent.com/pod-product-compliance
Lightning Source LLC
Chambersburg PA
CBHW051829180726
48283CB00004BA/1367